Generously donated by

Marilyn Carpenter
Children's Literature Professor
at EWU from 1998 to 2011

THE LIBRARIES
EASTERN WASHINGTON UNIVERSITY
CHENEY, WASHINGTON

Captain Snap
and the
Children of Vinegar Lane

by Roni Schotter
illustrations by Marcia Sewall

ORCHARD BOOKS
A division of Franklin Watts, Inc.
New York

Text copyright © 1989 by Roni Schotter
Illustrations copyright © 1989 by Marcia Sewall

ORCHARD BOOKS
387 Park Avenue South
New York, New York 10016

Orchard Books is a division of Franklin Watts, Inc.

Manufactured in the United States of America

Book design by Tere LoPrete

10 9 8 7 6 5 4 3 2 1

The text of this book is set in ITC Clearface Regular
The illustrations are done in a resist technique.

Library of Congress Cataloging-in-Publication Data

Schotter, Roni.
     Captain Snap and the children of Vinegar Lane/by Roni Schotter; illustrations by Marcia Sewall.
        p.   cm.
     Summary: The children of Vinegar Lane discover that bad-tempered old Captain Snap has a wonderful secret.
        ISBN 0-531-05797-6.   ISBN 0-531-08397-7 (lib. bdg.)
        [1. Friendship—Fiction.] I. Sewall, Marcia, ill. II. Title.
PZ7.S3765Cap 1989
[E]—dc19   88-22489
                                                                              CIP
                                                                               AC

To Jesse and Rich
—R.S.

To Stephanie, my godchild
—M.S.

Nobody liked to go to the end of Vinegar Lane. Captain Snap lived there, and everyone was afraid of him. He was thin and mean and bent and bitter. His skin was as cracked and as dry as a slice of stale bread.

People said Captain Snap lived like a rat, under a pile of old junk. Otto Phelps said his roof was only a piece of rusty tin, his walls were rotten bits of board nailed together. Penina Boyle said his chimney was nothing but a crooked stack of hollowed-out tin cans.

Once in a while, on days when they felt especially twitchy and wiggly, the children of Vinegar Lane would pinch each other and run up the street to spy on Captain Snap.

The bravest of the group was also the littlest. Her name was Emily Ann Crocker, but everyone called her Sody.

"Go ahead, Sody. Say something," the big kids would whisper, and little Sody would pop her head out from behind the grille of a rusty radiator and yell, "Come out, come out, Captain Snap."

And Captain Snap would come bumping, knocking, and crashing out of his house, scattering boxes and boards and bits of broken bottles in front of him.

"How you doing today, Captain Snap?" Sody would ask, her hands on her knees to keep them from knocking.

And no matter what the day, no matter what the hour, Captain Snap always did the same odd thing. He'd stamp his foot, snap his fingers, and pull his lip out so far that when he let go of it, it snapped back against his face with a "plap!" like the sound of rainwater hitting an empty bucket.

And Sody would grab Moe and Moe would grab Myrna and Myrna would grab Maxie and Maxie would grab Curly Jess and Curly Jess wouldn't grab anyone at all, he'd just bolt down Vinegar Lane with Moe and Myrna and Maxie and Sody racing and stumbling and tripping to keep up with him.

"Weren't scared a-tall, were *you*?" Curly Jess would say when they were safely at the other end of Vinegar Lane.

"Notabit," the others would answer, all except Sody, who'd squint up her eyes till they looked like tiny brown raisins and gaze at the sky like she was thinking big thoughts.

One gray day—when the killing frost had just come and turned the leaves on Vinegar Lane to mahogany and gold—the children of Vinegar Lane pinched each other, put on their mittens, and ran off once again to spy on Captain Snap.

"Come out, come out, Captain Snap," Sody called from behind a broken washing machine.

But *this* time, no one came.

"Call him again," Curly Jess whispered. "Louder!"

"Hey, Captain Snap! You in there?" Sody yelled.

Still no answer. Only a sound like quiet sighing. Was it the wind?

"Where do you think he is?" Maxie asked.

Sodie squinted up her eyes and gazed at the sky. "Inside," she announced with certainty. "Follow me."

And Sody advanced toward Captain Snap's house with Myrna, Moe, and Maxie following behind her and Curly Jess bringing up the rear. At the side of the house was a filthy window made from a porthole of an old ship. Sody wiped the dirt away with the sleeve of her jacket and peered inside.

"Look!" she whispered, and everyone crowded close.

Through the grimy glass, they could see
a room full of junk and Captain Snap lying, like a
pat of melted butter, droopy and yellow, on a stack
of old brown mattresses.

"He's dead," Myrna whispered, shaking her
head slowly.

"No way," Sody said. "Look at his breath."

Sure enough, a small puff of steamy gray
smoke hung in the cold air just above Captain
Snap's mouth.

"He's alive," Curly Jess announced. "But sick.
Real sick."

"And freezing," Moe added. "Look at his legs.
They got bumps on them like a raw chicken."

"No choice," Curly Jess said. "We gotta help."

Everyone nodded and turned to Sody.

"No choice," she said. "Come on!"

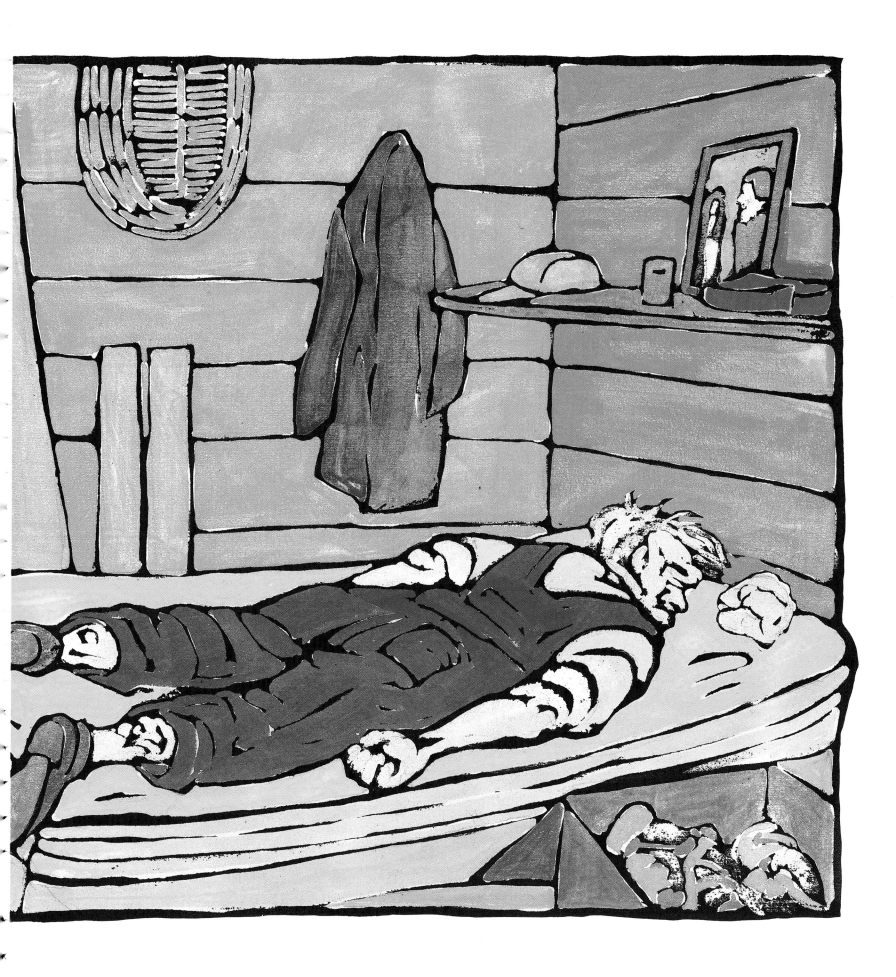

And late that afternoon—while a passing squall spit the first layer of snow dust on Vinegar Lane—the children of Vinegar Lane loaded Sody's red wagon with blankets and a pot of Sody's mother's homemade stew and took turns pulling it up Vinegar Lane to Captain Snap's house.

"Follow me," Sody said when they got there. She lifted the heavy stew pot and took many tiny quick steps toward Captain Snap's door. Behind her, Moe, Myrna, and Maxie tiptoed, each carrying a blanket, with Curly Jess hugging a red one and moving steadily in the opposite direction.

"I-I-I-I'll b-b-be the lookout," Curly Jess chattered. "I-I-I-I'll watch from the window."

Sody set the stew pot down in front of Captain Snap's door. Tap, tap, she knocked.

But no one answered.

RAP, RAP, she knocked again, louder.

"Captain Snap!" she called out.

Kerrrr-rash! Something fell inside.

"Look out!" Curly Jess cried. "Watch it! Here he comes!"

And from the other side of the door, they heard Captain Snap's sick voice, creaking like the hinge on a rusty gate. "Go away, scat! Be gone with you...."

The children of Vinegar Lane didn't wait to hear more. They just dropped their blankets and tore down Vinegar Lane with Curly Jess back in the lead.

Only Sody paused to look back, so only she saw two bony hands lift the stew pot into the dark interior of Captain Snap's house.

"It'll be a cold day in July before *I* go back there," Myrna swore.

"Same here!" everyone agreed.

But one week later, when the sky was as blue as a flower, they were back once again at Captain Snap's window.

"He's gone!" Curly Jess shouted. "This time I bet he really *is* d-d——"

Sody didn't stop to listen. She ran to Captain Snap's door with the big kids at her heels and was just lifting her fist to knock when, all on its own, the door swung open....

"W-w-what do-we-do-we-do-we-do-we-do n-n-now?" Curly Jess asked.

"We go *in*," Sody announced. She took an extra gulp of air and grabbed Moe and the others. All together, they pushed and squeezed their way through Captain Snap's door.